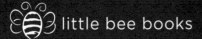

251 Park Avenue South, New York, NY 10010
Copyright © 2019 by Little Bee Books, Inc.
All rights reserved, including the right of
reproduction in whole or in part in any form.
Little Bee Books is a registered trademark of Little Bee Books, Inc.,
and associated colophon is a trademark of Little Bee Books, Inc.
Manufactured in the United States of America LAK 0419
ISBN: 978-1-4998-0852-0 (pbk)
First Edition 10 9 8 7 6 5 4 3 2 1
ISBN: 978-1-4998-0853-7 (hc)
First Edition 10 9 8 7 6 5 4 3 2 1
ISBN: 978-1-4998-0854-4 (ebook)

Library of Congress Cataloging-in-Publication Data
Names: Mae, Jamie, author. | Hartas, Freya, illustrator.
Title: Prank wars! / Jamie Mae, Freya Hartas.
Description: First edition. | New York: Little Bee Books, [2019] | Series: Isle of Misfits; 3 | Summary: Mythical creatures Gibbon, Ebony, Fiona, Alistair, and Yuri are assigned a mission to help a cyclops who is being bothered by trolls, but arrogant classmates are assigned to help the trolls.
Indentifiers: LCCN 2018053930 (print) | LCCN 2018057604 (ebook)
Subjects: | CYAC: Conflict management—Fiction. | Cooperativeness—Fiction. | Trolls—Fiction. | Friendship—Fiction. | Schools—Fiction.
Classification: LCC PZ7.1.M29 (ebook) | LCC PZ7.1.M29 Pr 2019 (print) | DDC [Fic]—dc23 | LC record available at https://lccn.loc.gov/2018053930

littlebeebooks.com

Isle of
MISFITS
PRANK WARS!

by JAMIE MAE
illustrated by FREYA HARTAS

little bee books

CONTENTS

——— CHAPTER ONE ———

A BABA YAGA, A TROLL, A GHOUL, AND A GREMLIN GET A MISSION

"**W**e just got the coolest mission ever!"

Gibbon stopped walking when he heard someone talking about missions. Gibbon and his friends went on their first mission to help another creature a month ago, and he couldn't wait to go on another one! Who else could have gotten a mission?

1

When he turned to look, he saw Lissa the baba yaga in the center of a group of classmates. Gibbon had just left his History of Cursed Jewels class with his friends. Even though they all stood on the steps of the school building, he seemed to be the only one who heard Lissa. Ebony, Fiona, and Yuri chatted about what they'd learned while Alistair nodded along.

Gibbon stepped a little closer to Lissa to hear what she was saying better.

"What do you get to do?" a harpy asked, flapping her wings around excitedly.

"It's top secret," Lissa said as she folded her arms and grinned.

"Fitzgerald said he couldn't trust anyone else with this!" added Gashsnarl the ghoul with a high five to Trom.

Gibbon rolled his eyes. Maybe they were telling the truth, but he remembered how their team acted during the obstacle course race a few months ago. Gibbon's team came in second place in the competition, but still won because Fitzgerald saw Lissa trip Gibbon at the very end. If they were playing fair and square, Gibbon was sure he and his friends would have won.

Why would Fitzgerald give them a secret mission? Gibbon wondered. So what if Lissa and Gashsnarl were some of the top students in their class, coming second only to Ebony? They were cheaters.

"What's wrong?" Yuri asked, nudging Gibbon.

"Lissa's bragging about a secret mission," he muttered.

Yuri frowned as he looked over at the crowd surrounding Gashsnarl and Lissa. "Really? They got a mission? How come we didn't get another mission?"

"We helped Declan not too long ago," Ebony said.

Gibbon looked to Yuri and knew his friend was thinking the exact same thing as him. Helping Declan the leprechaun find his gold had been *so* long ago. Since then, all they'd been doing was going to classes, classes, and more classes. He loved learning about so many new things, but he longed for the adventure of another mission, probably just as much as Yuri did.

Alistair sighed. "I do miss helping other creatures. Remember how happy Declan was when we found his gold? And when we helped Lachlan find his family? That was pretty cool."

"Lissa is just being a show-off, like always," Fiona said as she flapped her wings with attitude.

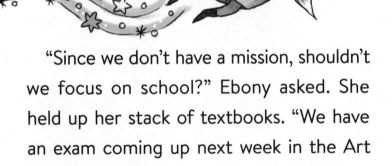

"Since we don't have a mission, shouldn't we focus on school?" Ebony asked. She held up her stack of textbooks. "We have an exam coming up next week in the Art of Bewitching."

Reluctantly, Gibbon nodded. His favorite part about being on the Isle of Misfits was all the books he got to read at the library. Their collection was so much bigger than the one at the castle he grew up in. His least favorite part of the Isle was tests, but with Ebony's help, he knew he'd usually pass them.

With one final look back at Lissa and Gashsnarl, Gibbon went with his friends to the ivy-covered library.

CHAPTER TWO

FITZ'S OFFICE

The next day, after classes were finished, Fitzgerald found Ebony and her friends and invited them into his office. Ebony was in awe over how organized Fitzgerald kept everything. Each book was alphabetized on his shelves by title and every piece of paper on his desk had a proper place. This was everything she dreamed her own dorm room would be, but Fiona was her roommate.

11

As much as she loved her fiery fairy friend . . . well, Fiona was a little tornado. All her quick flights around the room made papers go everywhere and she never, ever put books back in their proper place.

Gibbon plopped down in a chair in front of Fitzgerald's desk. Yuri and Alistair both sat down on a big couch, but Ebony and Fiona decided to stay standing—or in Fiona's case, flying.

"I have a mission for you," Fitzgerald said.

"A mission?!" Gibbon perked up in his chair.

"I knew it," Fiona said with a smirk. "What is it?"

"There's a cyclops who lives in the mountain on the other side of the island. Below the bridge leading to his cave, a pack of trolls have made themselves a home. The cyclops has been having problems with the trolls, and I'd like you to go and try to resolve them."

Ebony almost squealed with excitement. This was the very sort of mission she'd always wanted! She had aced her Conflicts & Conversations course last semester and would be able to use the skills she learned there to help the cyclops and the trolls.

As the team made their way to the other side of the island, everyone tried to guess what was wrong.

"The trolls are probably stinking up the whole mountain!" Gibbon said.

"I bet they are trying to make him solve a riddle every time he crosses the bridge," Yuri replied.

"Maybe they keep throwing parties and are being too noisy at night. Trolls aren't quiet," Alistair added.

"I bet the cyclops is the one causing trouble and we're the muscle Fitzgerald sent to make him behave himself!" Fiona said as she knocked her fists together.

Ebony laughed a little at that idea. She doubted that could be the case. She didn't try to guess during their journey to the other side of the island. There was no reason to—once they reached the cyclops, he'd tell them.

Instead, she enjoyed walking from the school buildings, past the wooden dorms with their garden-filled roofs, all the way across the training fields and beyond. A forest covered the north side of the island, and a mountain range was beyond that.

They walked through the forest and up one of the smaller mountains until they found the entrance to the cyclops's cave.

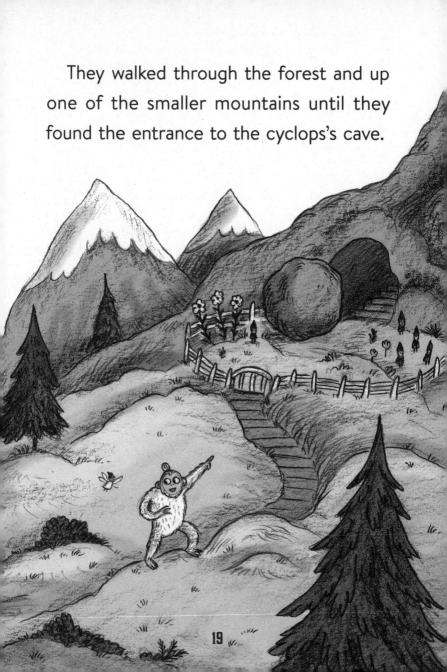

— CHAPTER THREE —

THE CYCLOPS'S CAVE

Alistair knocked on the side of the cave as Gibbon and Ebony wandered over to a little garden next to the entrance. Suddenly, they heard the thudding steps of something big coming toward them. Then, he was there.

Oh, wow! Fiona thought. The cyclops towered over them. And he was twice the size of Alistair! He was so tall that his head almost hit the ceiling. His whole body was squishy and his one, big eye looked over each of her friends until it stopped on her. *He's . . .*

he's

so big!

There were a lot of monsters at the academy bigger than Fiona, but not anything this big. She fluttered behind Ebony, glancing at the cyclops over her friend's shoulder.

He just has ONE eye, Fiona reminded herself. She had two good eyes. *I bet I can fly so fast, he won't see me!*

"Greetings! I'm Cyrus. Are you the group Fitz sent?" the cyclops asked.

"You mean Fitzgerald?" Ebony replied politely.

"Fitz and I go way back," Cyrus explained. "Come on in."

With his invitation, they entered the mysterious cave.

"This is so exciting," Ebony whispered to Fiona. "I've only ever read about a cyclops. I've never met one!"

"They're huge," Fiona muttered back.

"Whoa! This is so neat!" Alistair called out as he entered the living room. The furniture looked fancy, covered in royal purple velvet with gold patterns etched into the wood. Everything was perfectly placed, just like in Fitzgerald's office, which wasn't what Fiona was expecting at all. She thought a giant creature like a cyclops would have a messy home, not something that looked so . . . so nice.

"Can you tell us what's wrong?" Yuri asked. He barely looked around the home before getting straight to business. "Fitzgerald just said you had a problem with the trolls that live beneath the bridge near your cave."

"Yes," Cyrus said. "Oh, where are my manners? Would any of you like something to drink before I get started?"

The group happily accepted water after their long trek. When Cyrus went to the kitchen to get their drinks, Fiona darted around him quickly to find out whether he could see her. When he got out the glasses, she lingered on his right side, waving her hands to see if he would react. When he filled the glasses with water, she flew to his left side and made a funny face. Since he didn't seem to notice any of it, she guessed his vision wasn't that great. She trailed behind him as he walked back to the living room.

Fiona was the last one to get a glass of water when Cyrus passed them out. Once he handed her a tiny little cup, he smiled and said, "You are a quick little fairy, aren't you? Very energetic?"

She narrowed her eyes at him. "What do you mean?"

"All your flying around in the kitchen, making those faces and waving—did you think I didn't see you?"

Surprised, she almost dropped her glass. Okay, maybe his vision wasn't *that* bad.

"Thanks for the water," Alistair said. "Would you mind telling us about your trouble with the trolls?"

"Well, as you might have noticed, I don't have a door to my cave. There's a big boulder I can push in front of it, but that makes it hot inside and gives me no light during the day, so I keep it open. A month ago, I started to notice strange things happening.

One of my garden gnomes went missing. Then other small items around my home like books and slugs disappeared. Recently, it got worse. They started to play pranks on me. They . . ."

Cyrus's tan face turned a pinkish hue. "They . . . they put my underpants atop the mountain's flagpole. Then they loosened my salt shakers so when I used them, all the salt poured on top of my food and ruined it. And just yesterday, I found all the furniture in my bedroom upside down and stuck to the ceiling. Here, come and see for yourselves."

They put their drinks down on the table before following Cyrus further back into the cave. In the last room at the end of the hall, they each peeked in and saw exactly what he had described. His bed, along with his dresser, lamp, and a reading chair, were all stuck to the ceiling.

Gibbon suppressed a giggle, and Fiona whistled. "That's not easy to do."

"No, it isn't. Even for me, it'll take a while to get that stuff down." He rubbed his shoulder and frowned. "I slept on my couch last night. It wasn't very comfortable. After this last prank, I couldn't take it anymore, so I reached out to Fitz. Only the trolls could be doing this, I'm positive. So . . ." Cyrus turned back to them, a hopeful look in his eye. "Do you think you can help me?"

CHAPTER FOUR

TROLL TALK

Yuri thought the best way to handle this situation was by going to talk to the trolls. They all walked out of the cave and past the garden. Maybe they could talk some sense into the little tricksters and keep them from pulling any more pranks on Cyrus. On the walk down the mountainside, Ebony rambled on about all the things she learned in her Conflicts & Conversations course last semester. It was an advanced class, so of course, the only one in their group who had taken it so far was Ebony.

"Make sure to listen to both sides," Ebony said. "Don't accuse the trolls of anything. Be nice. Being mean won't get us anywhere, and it will just make them uncooperative."

"I've never met trolls before," Gibbon declared. "This will be so awesome!"

"Yes, you have," Fiona replied. "Remember Trom? The big, bald guy in Lissa's group? He's a troll."

Gibbon thought about it for a second. "Oh, yeah. You're right. I don't have any classes with him, so I never really see him."

"He's small for a troll," Fiona said. "I bet these bridge trolls are big!"

When they got closer to the bridge, Yuri had a feeling Fiona was right. They could feel the ground shaking and hear the sounds of laughter and music. Trolls, especially bridge trolls, were known for having fun. They liked to dance and listen to music, and they especially liked to trick people. So, these trolls playing pranks on their neighbor made sense to Yuri.

Before they got to the bridge though, another group crossed their path. Not just any group either, but Lissa, Gashsnarl, Trom, and their gremlin friend—Jori? Yuri was pretty sure that was the gremlin's name.

"Hey! What are you doing here?" Fiona asked as she flew up to be eye to eye with Lissa.

"We're on our mission," Lissa said proudly. "What are you guys doing here?"

"We're on a mission, too," Alistair said.

Lissa glanced over at Alistair before turning her attention to Gibbon. "Oh, yeah? What's your mission about?"

"Top. Secret." Gibbon grinned.

"That's not true," Ebony whispered. "Fitzgerald didn't say anything about—"

"You tell us about yours and we'll tell you about ours," Yuri interrupted.

Lissa thought this over for a second and exchanged a look with Gashsnarl. With a nod, Gashsnarl said, "We're helping some bridge trolls out. Their neighbor, a cyclops, has been stealing their stuff. He took some pots and pans from them. And lamps, too! It's even started to get worse. Now, he's playing pranks on them."

"What?" Ebony gasped.

"That's not true!" Fiona said. "Our mission is to help the cyclops because the bridge trolls are taking his things and playing pranks on *him*—not the other way around."

"Hey," Trom said, taking a step toward them. "My troll friends say they are the ones having things stolen! They're the ones telling the truth!"

"That's right, the trolls are innocent!" Lissa barked.

"No way, no how!" Fiona said crossing her arms.

"I saw the prank the trolls did myself," Gibbon argued.

"Well, I saw what the cyclops did to the trolls," Trom snapped.

"It doesn't matter what you guys say," Yuri said. "I know we'll get to the bottom of this and complete our mission."

Jori smirked. "No way. We'll finish our mission first."

CHAPTER FIVE

SPLITTING UP

"I have an idea," Alistair declared. His voice, though soft, was enough to stop the two groups from arguing. Slowly, each creature looked at Alistair.

"What's your idea, dragon?" Lissa asked.

"My name is Alistair," he said, annoyed.

Lissa should have known his name by now. "What if Gibbon and Ebony go with your team to help the trolls, and you and Trom come with Yuri, Fiona, and I to help the cyclops? You and Trom think the trolls are innocent, so you'll make sure we don't miss anything. And Gibbon and Ebony will make sure Gashsnarl and Jori don't miss anything, either."

Lissa watched Alistair carefully before looking to her friends. Jori and Gashsnarl looked at each other before shrugging, and Trom, with a huff, nodded. "Okay, we'll agree to that. But it'll only prove we're right and you're wrong."

"We'll see about that," Yuri said.

Alistair wasn't as sure as his friends were about what was true and what wasn't. If the trolls were having problems, they needed help, too. And at least this way, everyone would stop fighting and get to work to solve this problem.

Yuri, Fiona, Alistair, Lissa, and Trom all went back to see Cyrus. Trom and Yuri were silent on the way, both trying to be the leader of the new group. They walked faster than everyone else. Sometimes, Trom was ahead, and other times, Yuri.

"Boys," Lissa grumbled.

"For reals," Fiona said. The girls exchanged a look, then slowly smiled at each other and shook their heads.

Alistair was glad to see them agree on something, even if it was just on something small. Lissa and Fiona had always gotten into arguments at school. *Maybe this mission will change things*, he thought happily. Yuri and Trom kept racing to get to the cyclops's cave first, but Lissa and Fiona hadn't argued the whole time, so that was encouraging.

It was true Lissa cheated during the obstacle course challenge, but Alistair figured she'd learned her lesson. It had meant her team lost, so she probably wouldn't do it again. Besides, Lissa was like Ebony—at the top of their class. It was as important to her as it was to Ebony to stay that way. He could see how, even if it was wrong, Lissa might have thought it was a good idea at the time to trip Gibbon to stay on top.

As they walked through the garden outside of Cyrus's cave, Alistair paused to admire two shiny, red-capped gnomes that sat nicely between roses and daisies. He took a deep, deep breath—so deep that the colorful flowers swayed toward him. Sometimes, flowers smelled so good.

"Come on, Alistair!" Fiona called out as she entered the cave.

Quickly, he followed his friends.

"You're back!" Cyrus said.

"Hey, Cyrus! These are our classmates," Alistair explained, waving toward Lissa and Trom. "They heard the trolls' side of the story, and we thought it'd be good for them to hear your side, too."

"The trolls' side?" Cyrus frowned, looking directly at Trom. "Do you live under the bridge with them?"

Trom shook his head. "I live at the academy, not with the bridge trolls."

"Well, if Fitz sent you, then you must be okay," Cyrus said. "Did you see the bridge trolls on your way back here?"

"No, why?" Fiona asked with a tilt of her head.

"They stole more of my gnomes is why," Cyrus said with a lowered head. With a sigh, he led them back out to his garden and motioned to four patches in the ground where no grass had grown. "I used to have a whole pack of garden gnomes here, and now most of them are gone. What am I going to do?"

CHAPTER SIX

THE TROLLS UNDER THE BRIDGE

Gibbon and Ebony stuck together the whole way to the bridge. Gibbon wasn't sure what to think of Jori or Gashsnarl, or why Alistair thought this was a good idea. Their group of friends worked well together. They proved that during the obstacle course and when they found Declan's pot of gold, so why would Alistair want to mess that up by mixing the teams?

Jori was a hairy gremlin with bright green eyes. He kept glaring at Gibbon the whole way and it was freaking Gibbon out.

When they got to the bridge, it was the ghoul Gashsnarl who called down to the trolls. After a minute, the trolls stopped playing their music and stuck their heads up to see them.

"Gashsnarl!" one of the trolls called out with a smile. "Have you talked everything out with that cyclops?"

"Not yet," Gashsnarl grumbled. "These are our fellow students. They're looking into the same case we are—but they've already talked to the cyclops."

"Have you told him to return our pots and pans?" the troll asked. "We can't cook without them."

"We're hungry!" someone called out from below the bridge.

"We only have this one left," another troll said as he held up a small silver pan with a white handle. "Not nearly enough to cook food for everyone."

"We're also sick of him stealing our pants and setting them up on the bridge like flags!" another troll called out.

Gibbon frowned. "Well, maybe you shouldn't steal his underpants and hang them on the flagpole on top of the mountain."

The troll looked at Gibbon like he had said something awful. "Huh? We would never!"

"Have you also never gone into Cyrus's home and rearranged his furniture?" Ebony asked, but her tone was sweet and kind, so the troll didn't seem to take offense.

"We've never been inside his home. He's never invited us," the troll said.

"Not very friendly, that cyclops!" another troll called out.

"Told you so," Jori growled. "It's the cyclops, not the trolls."

"This is weird," Ebony said as she tapped her chin. "We should talk to Cyrus again. There seems to be more going on than we'd originally thought."

"Tell him to give us our pots back!" the troll said one last time before ducking back under the bridge.

When they made it back to the top of the mountain, the sky was turning all shades of orange and pink. They couldn't stay too long or else they wouldn't get back to the dorms before nightfall. Gibbon glanced at Ebony, who was looking up at the sky nervously. He knew she didn't like being out after dark.

"Night is the best, isn't it?" Gashsnarl
said as he smiled up at the sky.

"Why do you say that?" Gibbon replied,
even though he agreed. Back when he
lived at the castle, Gibbon had to stay still
during the day. It was only at night when
he was free to move around and explore
the area.

"Ghouls are night creatures," Gashsnarl
said. "Aren't gargoyles, too?"

"Yeah, we are." Gibbon nodded.

"It's hard to adjust to the daytime schedule at school, isn't it?"

"It is. And I do miss running around in the moonlight," Gibbon said longingly.

"Same." Gashsnarl sighed as they arrived at the cave.

Ebony knocked on the wall. Not too long after, Cyrus came out wearing a robe and had soap on top of his head. He had a loofah in one hand and a rubber ducky in the other.

"Oops, we didn't mean to interrupt your shower," Ebony said.

"No worries, little griffin," Cyrus said. "You missed your friends. They were here about a half hour ago, looking over the damage the trolls did."

"Do you mind if we come in again, and show our classmates Gashsnarl and Jori what's been happening?" Ebony asked.

Cyrus looked at the two new creatures and nodded. He showed them to his bedroom, but while Jori and Gashsnarl went to look, Gibbon lingered in the kitchen. In the sink, he noticed a pile of pots and pans that hadn't been there when they visited Cyrus earlier.

Looking closer, he saw each pot and pan was silver and had white handles, just like the pan he had seen at the trolls' place.

"What's wrong?" Ebony asked as she walked over with Gashsnarl and Jori trailing behind.

"These are the pots and pans from the trolls, right?" Gibbon said as he pointed to the sink.

"Told you it was the cyclops!" Jori said.

"What?" Cyrus came out from the back room, scrubbing his head free of soap with a towel. When he saw the sink, he jumped from surprise. "What are all those pots doing in there?! I just cleaned!"

"These belong to the trolls." Gashsnarl folded his arms and looked at Cyrus sharply. "Explain yourself, cyclops!"

"I've never seen them before in my life," Cyrus said. He went to his shelves and motioned toward his pots. "Look! All of my pots are copper, not silver."

Gibbon looked at the two different types of pots, and then back at Gashsnarl. "What if he's telling the truth?"

Gashsnarl watched Gibbon carefully for a moment. "They can't both be telling the truth . . . can they?"

Ebony frowned and said, "Could it be that they're *both* being pranked?"

CHAPTER SEVEN

PRANK WARS!

After a good night's rest back at the academy, the two groups met again in front of the dorms. Lissa leaned against the wooden building, twirling her long, dark hair around a finger as Ebony told the group what they had discovered at Cyrus's home last night.

"So you think someone is pranking both of them?" Fiona asked.

71

"It could be, I guess," Lissa added.

"I think it's the only thing that makes sense, isn't it?" Yuri scratched his head, looking to his friends for answers.

"If both of them are the victims here, we should all work together," Alistair suggested.

Gashsnarl, Trom, and Jori looked at Lissa. Gibbon knew it all came down to her—if she said no, then that would be that. But to his surprise, she looked to Fiona and smiled.

"Okay, sure," Lissa said. "Let's all work together."

Gibbon's mouth almost fell open when he saw Fiona smile back at Lissa. *When did those two become friends?* he thought.

"But if they're both being pranked . . . then who's doing the pranking?" asked Yuri.

"Let's go back to the mountain and search for clues," Fiona said.

As one big team, they did just that. Trom and Yuri still jumped ahead to lead the group, but it seemed more like a game than an actual race. Each time Trom got the lead, he'd grin back at Yuri and dare him to catch up—only for Yuri to laugh and egg on Trom when he did.

Jori, Ebony, and Alistair all talked about their favorite class—Mischief and Mayhem: 101—while Lissa and Fiona joked about something Gibbon couldn't hear. Gashsnarl walked beside Gibbon, watching the two groups with a weird look on his face. Finally, he turned to Gibbon.

"Do you think this was what Fitzgerald had planned the whole time?" he asked.

Gibbon shrugged. "What do you mean?"

"We have never really gotten along. He didn't need to assign both of us to this mission. And he is the smartest guy on the whole island. He had to know the trolls and Cyrus were both being pranked. What if he assigned the two groups to make us all . . . become friends?"

Now that Gashsnarl said that, it did sound like something Fitzgerald would do. Gibbon looked at the group walking ahead of him, everyone talking and laughing with each other.

"Well, if that was Fitzgerald's plan, it looks like it worked," Gibbon said with a smile. Gashsnarl grinned and when he started to chuckle, Gibbon couldn't help but join in.

They wanted to check in with the trolls on their way up the mountain, but it was still too early for them.

"Bridge trolls like to stay up late and sleep until at least noon," Trom explained.

So instead of waiting for them, the group kept going all the way up to Cyrus's cave. It was still pretty early, but Gibbon hoped he would be awake. However, when they arrived, the boulder still blocked the entrance. Yuri knocked, but the cyclops didn't answer.

They waited outside in his garden. *This isn't good! We're on our second day and we have no leads and no one to talk to . . . can we even solve this?* Gibbon worried.

"Hey," Ebony called out and waved the group over to join her. She pointed to the shiny, red-capped gnomes near the daisies and roses. "The gnomes are back."

"I don't get it. Why would someone steal garden gnomes?" Trom asked.

Ebony pulled out her notepad from her backpack and flipped through her notes. "Yep, just as I thought. There were only two in the garden yesterday. Four were missing."

"Why would someone bring them back?" Yuri asked.

Gibbon got closer. He looked the gnomes over, one by one, before breaking out into a big smile. Back at the castle, he had to stay still all day while people walked by below. He knew just what it looked like to try to do that. And these gnomes? They weren't garden gnomes. He was pretty sure they were real gnomes pretending to be as still as garden gnomes!

He bent down low to get on eye level with the gnomes and locked eyes with the one closest to him. The very hardest part about staying still all day was not blinking. Staring contests were the only game the other gargoyles would play at the castle, so Gibbon was a champ. This gnome didn't stand a chance!

Squatting down was starting to feel like hard work. Gibbon could feel his legs start to cramp and shake, but he stayed focused on the gnome's eyes. He didn't want to miss the gnome blinking, except . . . it was taking an awfully long time, wasn't it? Maybe they really were just garden gnomes, but then who was playing the pranks? Just as Gibbon really started doubting himself, the gnome squinted.

"Ah!" the gnome shouted in a high-pitched voice, closing his eyes and rubbing them with his tiny hands. "No fair, no fair!"

"They're alive!" Jori shrieked, jumping into Alistair's arms.

"We've been discovered! RUN!" cried out another gnome. The six gnomes scattered, but Lissa and Gashsnarl each snatched one up, while Yuri and Ebony quickly grabbed the other four.

"Oh no, you don't!" Lissa said, lifting her captured gnome off the ground.

"Gnomes are really mischievous creatures," Ebony explained. "Were you the ones causing all the trouble for everyone?"

"Not trouble," one of the gnomes said. "We were only having a bit of fun!"

"Not anymore!" Lissa said as she held the gnome up to her face. "Got it? It's not funny. The trolls and the cyclops are really upset with each other."

"It was just a game," a gnome muttered.

"Your game caused a lot of problems," Ebony said.

"Is that fun for you?" Alistair asked.

Each of the gnomes frowned and hung their head.

"We're sorry," one of the gnomes said. "We didn't mean for it to make anyone angry. We just wanted to play!"

"If that's what you wanted, all you had to do was ask," Trom said, shaking his head with a grin. "Trolls love games. We'll introduce you to them and Cyrus, so you can say you're sorry. You can ask them to play with you, and I think you just might get some new friends. How's that sound?"

The gnomes looked at each other and smiled.

"You've got yourself a deal!" said the tiniest gnome.

CHAPTER EIGHT

THE FEAST

Lissa and Trom carried the trolls' pots and pans down to the bridge with Fiona. They could hear music before they even saw the bridge.

"Hey, everyone!" Trom called out once they arrived.

"Our pots!" a troll replied.

"We figured out what was going on," Fiona said as Lissa and Trom gave the trolls their items back. "Turns out, Cyrus's garden gnomes were real gnomes and they were the ones pulling the pranks."

"Ah, gnomes," the troll said. "They're little troublemakers!"

"Apparently, they thought they were playing and didn't mean to upset anyone," Lissa explained.

"We have our pots back and no harm was done, so all is forgiven," the troll said.

"Cyrus wanted us to invite you to his cave for dinner. What do you say?" Fiona asked.

More of the trolls appeared from under the bridge. "Food? We'd love to!"

Gibbon and the rest of the members of the two teams were already at the cave, helping Cyrus prepare for dinner when Fitzgerald arrived. Not too long afterward, Fiona, Lissa, Trom, and the bridge trolls came barreling in.

Cyrus had a long dining table that fit everyone. Even the gnomes ended up joining the meal. Everyone was scattered around the table, gnomes and trolls and a cyclops and Fitzgerald and friends, all talking and joking together.

To Gibbon's surprise, Cyrus was a great cook. He made a huge amount of food—meats, swamp stew, buttery mashed potatoes, moss pie, and even freshly baked bread! When the gnomes were served a worm potpie, Gibbon gagged and had to look away.

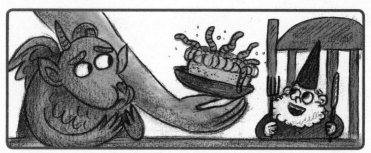

"You have a very nice place," one of the trolls said.

"Thank you," Cyrus replied. "I should have invited you all a long time ago. I'm sorry for all this mess."

"We are, too," the troll said.

"By the way, how did you manage to get Cyrus's furniture stuck to the ceiling?" Yuri asked the gnomes. "It's a good deal bigger than all of you."

"Ah, our finest prank," said a gnome. "All it took was a little bit of teamwork!" Everyone looked at each other and laughed.

Fitzgerald smiled as he watched everyone become friends before turning his attention to his students. "I'm glad to see you all managed to get along and solve this—together."

"I guess they're not that bad," Fiona said as she grinned at Lissa.

"Yeah, I guess so, too," Lissa replied.

Gibbon grinned as everyone began to dig into their food. He loved going on adventures, but this was the very best feeling—sitting at a table with new friends after completing another mission.

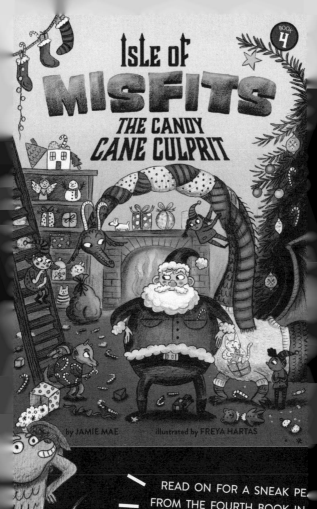

Isle of
MISFITS
THE CANDY CANE CULPRIT

by JAMIE MAE   illustrated by FREYA HARTAS

READ ON FOR A SNEAK PEA.
FROM THE FOURTH BOOK IN
ISLE OF MISFITS SERI

CHAPTER ONE

THE LEGEND OF SANTA

"**I**t's nearing that time of year again!" Mrs. Masry declared cheerfully.

Gibbon perked up at his desk and focused on his teacher, Mrs. Masry. She was a sphinx with the head of a human and the body of lion, so it was hard to miss her as she walked around the room.

"Since Christmas is around the corner, I thought today's lesson should be on creatures and mythology surrounding the holiday." She clicked her slider and an image of an old lady on a broomstick appeared. "In Italy, this is called La Befana. Much like Santa Claus, she flies around rewarding good children with gifts and candy, while bad children get coal. Though humans might not believe so, La Befana is not really different from a normal witch. This was just something she did to help Santa out before people started noticing her flying around on a broomstick and panicked!"

With another click, her slider changed to reveal a big, hairy creature with wicked horns. Gibbon cringed—whatever that creature was looked so mean, he never wanted to meet one.

"This is a much more well-known creature from Germany, the Krampus. To date, a Krampus has not been found, but legend has it—"

The door to the classroom opened, cutting Mrs. Masry off.

Fitzgerald poked his head into the room. "Hello, Mrs. Masry. Would it be alright with you if I borrowed Gibbon and Alistair?"

"Of course!" Mrs. Masry replied brightly. "Go ahead, boys."

Alistair and Gibbon glanced at each other nervously as they got up. Gibbon didn't think they'd done anything wrong lately.

Ebony, Yuri, and Fiona were already in the hallway. When Gibbon saw them, excitement built up in his chest like a burst of bats. This wasn't about being in trouble, this was about a mission!

"What's going on? I'm missing class!" Ebony said anxiously.

"Your team has been making quite a stir lately," Fitzgerald began. "Declan and Cyrus were very pleased with your work and talked you up to all their friends. Word got around, and a very special someone has requested your help."

"Really?" Fiona said with wide eyes.

"Yeah!" Yuri cheered, high-fiving Alistair—or at least, he tried. Alistair missed Yuri's hand and almost fell forward, but Yuri caught him so he didn't hit the ground.

"Who?" Gibbon asked.

"This is a very high priority, very top secret mission," Fitzgerald whispered as he looked around the hallway. "I can't talk about the specifics here. Word cannot get out about this trouble, or it would cause a panic."

A panic? Top secret mission? A very important someone requesting them? Gibbon bounced with excitement. This mission was going to be something special!

JAMIE MAE is a children's book author living in Brooklyn with her fluffy dog, Boo. Before calling New York home, she lived in Quebec, Australia, and France. She loves learning about monsters, mysteries, and mythologies from all around the globe.

FREYA HARTAS is a UK-based illustrator specializing in children's books. She lives in the vibrant city of Bristol and works from her cozy, cluttered desk. Freya loves to conjure up humorous characters, animals, and monsters and to create fantastical worlds and places for them to inhabit and get lost in.

Journey to some magical places and outer space, rock out, and find your inner superhero with these other chapter book series from **Little Bee Books!**

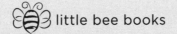